D1742185

Barry and 4 Part 2's

Alun Davies

Hi Maggie
Congratulations and best
wishes from the author.

June '21

Copyright © 2020 by Alun Davies

All rights reserved. No part of this publication may be reproduced, distributed, or transmitted in any form or by any means, including photocopying, recording, or other electronic or mechanical methods, without the prior written permission of the publisher, except in the case of brief quotations embodied in critical reviews.

ISBN:

978-1-9997855-3-6 (Paperback)

978-1-9997855-2-9 (E-book)

Illustrations by Klaire de Lys

All the quotes preceding each story are extracts from "Underneath the Fairy Teeth" by Ticking Tree

This is a work of fiction. Names, characters, places, and incidents either are the product of the author's imagination or are used fictitiously. Any resemblance to actual persons, living or dead, events, or locales is entirely coincidental.

Table of Contents

01

Barry and a Game of Stones

"Everyone's got some fog in their hand
As they go from the land to the sky through the wind
and the sand
They're all sharing the song but not hearing the band,
You must see jeopardy in that way
It means nothing today as you walk through the door
You make sure of your say in good time
What appears in your head
Is likely to stay."

Part 1

Barry liked playing Spider Stones and, for those of you who
may be unaware, I should begin by taking a moment to explain
how the game is played because it becomes very relevant later
in this story.

It is normally played by 12 "Stoners" at a time, that seems
to be the number which works best. Finding participants isn't
a problem; there are always Spiders hanging around and all of
them love games. Stones is usually played in the late evening
or at night, when there is less chance of interruption by people,
and it needs no special equipment. The dark isn't a problem

either because vibrations are used as the main means of detecting movement. Not all Spiders have very good eyesight, but for this game, they can see well enough.

Each Spider uses a different stone for the purpose of identification, which must be pre-registered with, and examined by, a judging committee; various shapes and sizes are used. Some Spiders have a favourite, jealously guarded stone to accommodate the way they wish to play, taking into account their own size and weight; however, whatever is available will do.

A square of nine inches is formed on the ground using multiple web threads fastened in place, and the stones for the game are placed inside the square and on the threads. Next, the Spiders form a circle, about a foot wide, around the square. Then, rather like the hokey cokey, they charge into it on a given signal with the objective of standing on their own stone, at which point they are pronounced by a judge as "safe". The Spider is then free to dismount and move rival stones out of the square before its owner has "stood", thus eliminating him or her from the game.

You can imagine that many legs in such a small space leads to a good deal of tripping, barging and shoving. Indeed, the whole thing sometimes gets very heated. The threads are already somewhat sticky and every player is able to make fresh ones as the contest develops. On average, it usually takes less than a minute before each Spider "stands" or a stone is "out". Only those that have "stood" qualify for the next round until eventually the final is played between the remaining 2 players. It is all very exhausting.

In the beginning, the most useful skills are speed and agility, but as the numbers reduce, other assets such as size, strength and strategy become more useful. All in all, a range of talents and tactics are needed in order to excel, and some Spiders are naturally much better at the game than others.

However, the ultimate objective of Stones is not winning or losing. Spiders believe that each competitor should gain something from it. So the real aim is self-improvement, particularly getting better at moving quickly, being aware of one's surroundings, adapting to developments and coping with changed circumstances. Everything is directed at becoming a better Spider.

Against that background, and to understand what I am about to explain, you should ideally also know about the real world of Spiders. I have described it elsewhere, so I will not repeat every detail. Suffice to say that Barry was likely to be one of a very special group of Spiders called Secrets. They are given certain powers that develop and strengthen over time. He had already been able to write a Magic Song and master some easy spells, but even so, he wasn't yet convinced he was anything out of the ordinary.

Barry always played the game of Stones like an ordinary Spider, so usually didn't do all that well. He was young and rather small so the physical aspect became harder to handle after three or four rounds. Nonetheless, he was sometimes the last one standing, and thus the winner, because of his ability to change strategy quickly by taking into account the remaining players and their preferred tactics.

It didn't really matter though; the important thing was improvement. Every Spider was content if lessons could be learned.

There was, however, an exception to this approach within the group of regular local Stoners; his name was Roger. To him, winning was everything and the purpose behind the game meant nothing. He and Barry were not on the best of terms.

I must now introduce you to another Spider; her name is Marie. Just like Roger, she lived next door at 16 Louvain Terrace, but while he preferred the comforts of life inside the house, she stayed in the garden as much as possible.

All three went to the dance classes held every other Wednesday evening at the doctor's surgery. Tensions reached a high point when Roger tripped Barry just as Marie was gliding gracefully by. Consequently, Barry barged into her, setting off a chain of collisions in the Spider Trot formation and leaving him red-faced with embarrassment.

"Why did you do that?" Barry demanded, glowering at Roger.

"I stumbled," answered Roger, grinning broadly. "No harm done! Accidents will happen."

"I'm so sorry," Barry turned and stammered an apology to Marie, helping her back onto her legs.

"It's not a problem," she replied, brushing herself down and giving Barry a warm smile.

Barry was totally unimpressed with Roger's explanation; he knew it hid the truth.

Luckily, there were only two places where they came into regular contact – the dance class and when playing Stones. Roger was a bigger Spider with some obvious talent and often won the local knock-about games; yet, his size was a bit of a problem when it came to dancing. He lumbered around looking terribly ungainly, whilst Barry moved as smoothly as web thread.

You may already know there is good and bad in all things. In every species, both of these characteristics exist side by side, and it is no different with Spiders.

Barry knew that Roger was a Coloured Spider, and this is a name I should explain in more detail.

Such Spiders have existed for thousands of years. Their name has absolutely nothing to do with an external colour, which would be a rather silly concept, and anyway, they look just like every other Spider. Instead, they are regarded as such because some of their normal Spider instincts have been influenced by unkind and selfish tendencies. Just like Secrets, they are unknown to others but are far more common in number, being found once in ten thousand and one Spiders. Although constrained by the teachings of The Chronicles, they bend, flex and interpret the rules of acceptable behaviour to favour their own ambitions.

Coloured Spiders are meant to exist, and like all facts, it must be respected. So, Barry only wanted to use Roger as another means to improve himself. He had no thought of taking things further, even though his early powers could have made Roger look foolish.

But when Roger put others at risk the situation became unacceptable; it started with Marie.

She liked the look of Roger. His size and swagger suggested an air of security, and he was an especially smooth talker. We should all beware of such creatures.

Barry noted Marie's feelings with dismay. At every dance class, he saw her falling deeper and deeper under Roger's influence, but there was no cause for him to intervene.

Then one day, by chance, he was in the garden at number 16 and overheard them talking; it changed his approach.

"I want to sing you a special song," Roger was saying, "but not now when everyone can listen. Will you meet me later under the moon dark? I can come out here again."

She readily agreed, but Barry wasn't happy. He instinctively knew something bad was underway.

Early that evening, as Roger strode along the garden path, Barry was watching undetected. When he didn't want to be seen, he could be practically invisible.

He saw them settle down and, after a moment or two, Roger began to sing.

The opening line of the song was, "One in ten thousand and one in ten thousand and one in ten thousand and one". It was about the exciting life of a Coloured Spider.

"That's lovely," said Marie when he finished, although because many of the words and phrases were confusing, she felt compelled to add, "but what does it mean?"

Roger came closer and closer to her. "Well, my dear, I didn't write that song. It has been around for a long time, but the messages are really rather clear. Many important things in life involve a number and, to certain Spiders, the most special of them is 10,001. Listen carefully, you may have heard of my abilities?"

"Er, no…not really," answered Marie.

"Ah," he looked disappointed. "Anyway, they are appreciated in some quarters, but never mind that for now. The local Spider Feet festival is tomorrow, but what you don't know is that Spiders like me have, over many years, won such competitions 10,000 times. Soon, it will be 10,001. It marks the beginning of a new era."

"Are you saying you're going to win? How do you know?" asked Marie, trying to understand what he meant. "Stones isn't an easy game."

Roger had moved so close that he only needed to whisper. "Don't worry, my victory is assured, and it brings me, and you, certain opportunities. But I shall need your help."

"Help? In what way? What can I possibly do?" Marie was puzzled.

Barry was also listening carefully. Roger was talking about a Stones game that was at a level above those usually played. Expert Stoners came from far and wide to play and be seen at Spider Feet events, and being so bold as to predict success was a display of outstanding confidence.

It became clear to Barry that not enough attention had been given to many deserving things, such as what actually causes a victor to be the winner. It was another lesson in life he would need to consider.

There was also the comment about help from Marie resulting in future opportunities. It indicated that Roger had already reached a certain level of knowledge and influence within the ranks of Coloured Spiders. He was, however, like Barry to some extent, yet to see the bigger picture beyond Louvain Terrace.

Marie always attended Spider Feet. She didn't play herself but took the chance to see the games, meet old friends and make new ones. There were updates available about any developments in Spider Land, information on changes in people's behaviour (a subject endlessly interesting to Spiders), and many side shows to watch and enjoy. Entertainment was provided by Spider bands and singers, and it was certainly a night of fun that was eagerly awaited. So, her own knowledge and experience told Marie that Stones was not the sort of game where the outcome could be predicted.

"How can you be so confident you'll win?" she asked again.

"It's because of what I am about to tell you. It's why I brought you out here tonight."

He got no further. The resident garden frog called Hermes had, like Barry, been watching and was now eyeing them with a hungry-looking expression. There are times when frogs eat Spiders and because it is the natural way of the world, the practice is respected and tolerated.

In their defence, Spiders had learned to sense when anything that might cause them harm came near, but Marie was so fully focused on Roger she had become vulnerable to predators. Her guard was down.

However, Roger recognised the danger and positioned himself on the other side of Marie, who had her back to Hermes. If a Spider was to be eaten, it wouldn't be him.

Roger could have given a warning but didn't; such a lack of care for others was totally unacceptable.

Barry quickly placed a sticky spell on Hermes, which meant his mouth wouldn't open. The poor frog began jumping around in frustration and then sat down, unsuccessfully trying to prise his lips apart.

Losing all interest in a potential supper, he soon hopped miserably away.

Roger saw Hermes leave without fully realising what had happened. Yet, he was aware of the possibilities. Coloured Spiders know when a spell is cast nearby. They couldn't know who it had come from, but it did indicate the presence of a Secret, and Coloured Spiders hate Secrets.

Roger looked around anxiously.

"What's the matter?" Marie asked, blissfully unaware of the situation.

"Nothing, but I must go back inside," said Roger, making a very quick departure.

"There's someone I need to see," he added, scurrying up the path.

How strange, thought Marie as she watched him go, *and how interesting*.

Part 2

Roger wanted to speak with Antoinette, the cat owned by his people-family. It is a mistake to think that Antoinette is an unusual name for a cat simply because you have not heard it before. Neither should you be surprised that Spiders can talk to cats; expectations can be misleading.

Anyway, Antoinette had a reputation, within the Spider residents at number 16, for being able to interpret the past and foretell the future.

Roger explained to her what had happened in the garden.

"I knew it," she said, with an air of knowledge and authority. "A Secret is definitely around here somewhere. There was that strange business of the Magic Song which everyone started singing. Since then, Charlie has practically been living in Louvain Terrace although his house is in Gibbons Villas. Cats like Charlie don't change their habits for nothing; something is drawing him here. So, I'm pretty sure from what you've told me that a Secret cast a sticky spell on poor old Hermes, although I do wonder why it interfered."

"Are you sure there's a Secret involved?" asked Roger. "I know you and Charlie are always fighting. You could be reading too much into things."

Antoinette smiled. "We only fight when he strays into my garden. We get on perfectly well most of the time and, I must say, Charlie does have a rare intuition for some things that even I don't have. You could ask him for a fuller explanation, but it definitely sounds like a sticky spell to me and that indicates a Secret."

She looked closely at Roger and added, "A Secret using his powers would be impossible to beat in a game of Stones."

Ignoring the last remark, Roger asked, "How can I find out who it is?"

But Antoinette had already stretched back into apparent slumber, with little time to spare for further conversation. She contributed all she wanted to the exchange with a last remark.

"You can never tell."

What neither Antoinette or Roger knew was that Barry had followed Roger into the house and was listening carefully.

Roger had plenty to consider if a Secret was in the area and taking an interest in his affairs. He'd seen the situation with Hermes so it was definitely a strong likelihood, but who was it?

After running through the possibilities, Roger narrowed the choice down to four candidates; Barry was not on the list. It goes to show how well Secrets can stay hidden. Roger returned to one of his favourite spots behind the front room curtains to think it all through.

Barry was also wondering how best to proceed. He was very wary of encouraging any talk of Secrets but knew Antoinette said things and gave advice with no basis in fact, truth or reality. There are those who will say whatever it takes to impress, and unfortunately, there are others who are inclined to believe what they hear. The lesson you should remember is to be careful who you trust.

Anyway, Barry concluded that he would also need to speak with Antoinette, and so when she left the house later that night he was waiting. In order not to arouse suspicion he simply asked for her opinion on what he'd seen earlier in the garden. Roger had already sought advice on the subject so a similar question from another curious and worried Spider was not unexpected.

They held a long conversation in which she did most of the talking. It proves the value of asking the right questions and then being a good listener.

The next morning he sought out Marie, who was strolling around trying to take her mind off Roger.

"Hi, Marie," he began.

"Barry, to what do I owe this honour?" she said.

"I need no special reason for wanting to see you, Marie, but as it happens, I do have something important to say."

The information he provided was, considering the circumstances, as simple and honest as possible. It left no doubt about the future and her role in it.

Later that day Spiders started to gather for the Spider Feet event. Everyone was enjoying a happy party atmosphere, and after much dancing, festivity and general merriment, it was time for Stones.

Because this was a major competition, many more than 12 Spiders had entered. Accordingly, there were a number of games to determine the finalists and Barry concentrated really hard to make sure he always qualified. Indeed, the more knowledgeable spectators thought he had never played so well.

Yet Roger remained the hot favourite to win and, like Barry, cruised through to the final without any trouble.

The garden shed Spiders were enjoying the festivities and talking about Stones. Barry's performance was the main topic of conversation.

"He's playing well, don't you think?" remarked Splash.

"I admit he's moving even quicker than normal," answered Emery, "but it looks to me like no one can move his stone. The Spider from number 18 nearly did himself a mischief when he tried, and Lawrence gave it a kick which almost broke his front leg."

"I hadn't noticed," said Sinbad. "Let's hope Barry wins, although it's not very likely. Roger is looking good and strong. I expect he'll finish on top and be crowned the last Spider standing."

"You have to understand that although the unexpected seems to sometimes happen, in reality, it never does. What happens is always expected."

Wondering who was speaking, the friends turned to see a Spider they'd never seen before.

"Excuse me," said Emery politely, although he was somewhat taken aback, "but isn't that just what we said? We all expect Roger to win."

"Yes, I heard. The future isn't a concept that's hard to talk about, but it's never properly explained. The unexpected can be stopped, the expected cannot; so that is what will happen," came the reply.

"What are you saying? How is the unexpected stopped?" asked Sinbad.

"Without you knowing. It must be that way. Otherwise, what happens would not be expected. Consider the matter more carefully. You think what you say or do or see is from an idea, action or thought of your own, but it is not so. All words, visions or movements started elsewhere, long ago."

"From where?" wondered Emery. "Surely what I do or see or say begins with me?"

"I cannot tell you too much, but as an example, take this game of Stones, which is the reason I came here today. You think Roger is expected to win, but you're wrong because he won't; that explains everything and so I can leave."

"Roger is the firm favourite, so why won't he win?" questioned Splash.

"...and why leave without seeing the end of the game?" added Emery.

"Because the unexpected is now expected and so I have no reason to stay. To know what will happen you must do more than watch. It is a requirement meant to constrain, but there are those who have no restrictions," came the reply.

Sinbad didn't look convinced.

"What does that mean? Who knows what the future holds?" he asked.

"Let's just say that Roger is a favourite who is not in favour," the Spider replied.

"He looks like the winner to me," Splash stubbornly maintained.

"That's because you rely on what passes through your eyes, so you cannot know what to expect," said the stranger who started to walk away then paused.

"Think of it this way; if a leaf fell from a tree but no one saw it fall, then when did it move? The answer comes from having looked at the tree, not seeing the leaf on the ground because time is then standing still. The clues are in motion, neither in the same place nor from the same source. Many are false, appearing where they will and given to more than your eyes."

"Wait," said Emery, "so are you saying you see and hear things we don't?"

But the Spider had left and would soon be far away.

"Who are you?" shouted Sinbad.

"I'm in disguise with nothing to hide," came the reply, travelling easily on the wind.

The friends watched him depart.

"I don't think we need to worry about his opinion very much," Emery said turning back to the others, but speaking in a loud, dismissive tone he hoped might still be heard.

It did, indeed, gain a distant, final response.

"I have no opinion. I rely on greater information."

The friends turned to look, but the Spider had gone.

"What was that all about?" asked Sinbad uneasily. He was well travelled and knew there were many unexplained things in the world.

"Beats me. I've never seen him before," said Emery.

Splash agreed, "He's not from around here."

For a short while, they debated what they had heard. It got them no further, and they resolved to say nothing more about it.

Roger had been watching the Spider Stone heats very carefully and noted how successfully Barry was playing the game. He thought about what Antoinette had said, and in the break before the final approached the judges with a claim that Barry was cheating.

This was a huge accusation in Spider Land which went completely against the objective of self-improvement. Indeed, it threatened the very concept of being a Spider. Nonetheless, Roger thought his success depended on Barry being disqualified. He needed to win and addressed the judges accordingly.

"I fully realise this is a big thing to say, but you've all seen what's happened. Barry's stone must be weighed down with something because it never moves an inch."

The Judge Jeffrey was in charge. Except for Spider Feet and important local meetings, he only occasionally left the middle of the grand web he had built under the arches of a bridge spanning a small river at the bottom of Louvain Terrace. It was why he was known as the Hanging Judge. There were two other junior judges present, Ken and Margaret.

Roger was waving his legs about and talking in an increasingly agitated tone.

"No one can move his stone! It's completely unnatural and totally against the spirit of the game. I demand he's disqualified and that I'm declared the winner."

The Judge Jeffrey looked grave.

"Be careful what you say, young Spider. Accusing a fellow competitor of cheating is a serious claim with many potential consequences. Barry's stone was properly registered and inspected in accordance with the rules. Nothing amiss was noted."

"So what?" Roger retorted. "Facts are facts. Something has happened after registration."

The judges conferred, and Barry was called upon for comment.

The Judge Jeffrey repeated the allegations from Roger.

Barry heard the charges and replied calmly and innocently.

"My stone can be moved as easily as any other. I would never cheat."

"No, that's not true," Roger maintained doggedly.

"Well, this is easily settled. Come and try," Barry said, motioning to the judges. They all trooped off to find out the truth of the matter.

There were only 2 stones in the circle and Barry lifted his up into the sky.

"That doesn't count," shrieked Roger. "I'm sure he can move it. It's everyone else who can't."

So, the Judge Jeffrey tried; he could lift it easily, as could Ken and Margaret.

Poor Roger. He looked mesmerised. He pushed his way forward and tried for himself; he raised it without difficulty.

"I don't understand this at all," he muttered, scowling deeply. "Look, ask Lawrence or Sid from number 18. They couldn't move it in the heats. I watched them try."

Both competitors were summoned.

"Lawrence?" said the Judge Jeffrey.

Lawrence shuffled forward, one of his legs was freshly bandaged.

"I didn't really attempt to move it," he said. "I more or less stumbled and sort of banged into it. I was concentrating on another stone and that one got in the way."

"I see," said the Judge Jeffrey with a nod. "Sid, what do you have to say?"

"Well, I did try to move it I suppose, but something told me my body wasn't quite right at that moment and, if I strained too hard, I might hurt myself. I eased off there and then. I'm sure I could have moved it out of the square otherwise."

Roger suddenly interrupted, "Look, I've just realised something. Barry is the Secret I've been told about. There is definitely one around here somewhere. He put some sort of spell on that stone, making it impossible to move by others during the game."

The Judge Jeffrey looked solemnly at Barry. He knew Secrets existed and had special powers.

"Is it true?" he asked.

Barry looked the Judge Jeffrey straight in the eye. It was a difficult moment because he could not reveal himself to be a Secret, which he wasn't sure about anyway, so he gave a limited reply.

"I have not placed any sort of spell on my stone nor caused one to be made. I repeat that I would never cheat or tell lies," he said.

Roger wanted to argue some more, but the Judge Jeffrey stopped him.

"We've heard all we need to hear, I think," he said wisely. "Leave us alone to consider our ruling, which will be based on the evidence."

The decision was never in doubt. To falsely accuse a fellow Spider of cheating was unforgivable, so Roger was banned from playing in all Stones competitions for 2 years. It was regarded as a very stern punishment.

Barry was declared the winner.

"I won't forget this!" Roger said angrily.

"Good. I hope you don't," answered Barry. "It may improve you."

Roger watched the prize-giving ceremony before storming out of the garden; we shall hear more of him in other tales.

As far as this story is concerned, you only need to know what happened to cause Roger's downfall.

Barry had asked Hermes to be in the garden when Roger and Marie were meeting. If the circumstances so warranted, he would put a harmless short sticky spell on him so that, in the confusion, Marie wouldn't hear the final thing Roger intended to say. Some words are best kept completely away from the innocent. There is no gain in everyone knowing what can cause harm; no good can come of it.

Hermes had readily agreed. He held Barry in high regard because of the way Barry had solved a tricky family problem he once faced, and which is the subject of yet another tale I may tell you one day.

The stranger who had spoken with Sinbad, Splash and Emery was more than a Secret and, unbeknown to Barry, had exercised three spells.

The first ensured Barry and Roger were kept apart in the heats. The second placed a heavy spell on Barry's stone, effective until he qualified for the final and making it immovable by the other competitors. Finally, Roger would conclude that the only way he could win was through Barry being disqualified.

I'm sure you are wondering what Barry said to Marie, but some words cannot be repeated, discussed or explained to others. All you need know is Barry began by saying he'd been to see Antoinette and before long Marie realised Roger was a Spider to be avoided.

Is that enough to satisfy your curiosity? Perhaps people have more in common with Spiders than they think. Why not simply remember that the expected always happens? It is overly complex to imagine it any other way.

Yet, I will add something more. I cannot break confidences, but I suppose there are some further generalities of interest that I can add.

Barry used much of what he'd heard from Antoinette. Speaking with her first had been necessary in terms of both credibility and confidentiality. The Spiders at number 16 believed she could see the future and it was something Barry could use to his advantage.

It meant he could tell Marie what she needed to hear. He explained how she would always be unhappy with a Spider whose name started and ended with the same letter. She had only to master time and she could expect better opportunities to appear in her life; everyone needs patience in such things.

As he placed his newly awarded trophy on the shelf in his little home under the kitchen sink, Barry reflected on the connections which made this story possible. There is much more to learn from understanding why many related threads could not, and cannot, be imagined but exist anyway.

It is a fact that must be accepted because nothing is only a beginning; you wake up in the morning because you went to sleep at night. The same truth is the key to knowing why the unexpected can never happen. If you think differently, then you have been deceived or are deceiving.

The information provided by Antoinette was, of course, completely bogus. Words can deceive you, but they must sometimes be heard in order to be useful. Barry could not begin a lie but could connect it when the circumstances were suitable.

You will need to read elsewhere to learn about some of the laws by which Spiders govern themselves. Without that understanding, the meaning of this story may still be unclear, but it has now been explained and contains whatever truth you think it does.

A Super Secret had been given a Revelation. Finally, the underlining could disappear and the Super concerned had travelled to Louvain Terrace for the Spider Feet gathering.

The Revelation became Chapter 7, Paragraph 18, of The Chronicles.

"The way ahead will forever be confusing and contradictory until the connections available for guidance are made and understood. Only action taken on this basis can have meaning, else it will be unhappy and uncertain. Everything takes part in providing information, no matter whether it is passive, powerful,

*past, present, true or false; nothing stands aside. It means
there are many influences to be considered in reaching the
expected result. The factors concerned cannot be counted
but can be counted upon. The most obvious are quickly
applied but all must take their place."*

It provided Barry with further words necessary for Marie to
hear at the time given for the telling.

As you grow, and if you are to improve, the knowledge you
gain or are given is completely unimportant; all that matters is
the knowledge you use.

02

Barry and the Mystery Web

"Seems to me, secretly, I can do what I want
Though I know in my soul it's not true
Could possess all that's best from a moment passed by
Nonetheless, if it's gone,
Then we got to move on."

Part 1

This is a tale that shows how nothing is impossible and amazing things have actually happened. In fact, they happen all the time but fail to be recognised.

This is how it began.

"Can't you make more space?" Barry heard Mother ask Father.

Barry knew it was impossible.

Space cannot be increased; it is what it is. The concept of adding space to space helped Barry realise people knew very little about the world.

From Mother's perspective, it was all very simple. The family was going on holiday and extra room was required in their car. They were going to Wales for a short break and not enough room could be found for everything she wanted to take.

"We're only going for a few days," complained Father. "Why on earth is all this stuff necessary?"

"Because you never know," said Mother. "The weather there is unreliable at best, and we'll need to smarten up a bit if we eat out somewhere. It's better to be safe than sorry."

"But surely there's no need to take the kitchen sink?" Father moaned. "Honestly, you'd think we were emigrating."

Still, he got on with the packing and re-packing, carrying various items and bags from the house to the car, and occasionally back from the car to the house. If you've ever been away, you'll know what it's like; for some reason, most mothers feel compelled to take more than could possibly be needed.

Leaving all those domestic arrangements aside for a moment, it was the destination that had piqued Barry's attention. He knew Wales was the best country on earth to make and find history. It was a place where even the smallest triumph in any possible field of endeavour could immediately become folklore. The country was so intriguing in general that Barry had always wanted to visit, and a particular historical episode always sparked his keenest possible interest.

However, before I say more about that, you should know that not all of the family fancied a road trip.

Jessica surveyed the cramped area where she would be sitting in total dismay. She believed that more space was certainly needed.

"Why on earth are we doing this?" she asked Mother wearily.

"Because we haven't been anywhere for a while, and your Father and I fancied driving to somewhere new on this island of ours. There's so much to see and learn."

Mother was feeling somewhat impatient with Jessica, who was at an age where friends and their opinions were her essential keys to happiness. Teenage years can be a troublesome period, although not always understood as such in passing through them. Thankfully with time a wider and better perspective usually appears.

Looking into the car, Jessica was still remarkably unimpressed and tried a different approach.

"We usually go skiing," she muttered; it made little useful impact.

"Well, we're not going skiing. It's time you appreciated some new things. Not everyone goes abroad, you know."

Mother had decided upon things so that was that and, as it so happens, Father was also keen.

"Good idea," he said when the idea was originally floated. "I'm fed up with airports. It'll be great to please ourselves, go where we want and do what we want when we want to do it. The kids should experience something different."

The matter was settled, dates were fixed and reservations were made; only the thorny issue of "space" remained a problem.

Father had a particular reason for wanting to go. His sketchy family history indicated a grandfather from West Wales. Confirmation came in a communication sent by distant relatives in Pennsylvania who were trying to trace the Davies family's origins. The details they provided went even further backwards into mid-Wales but their letter, together with a basic diagram of the family tree, stopped at a place called Trefeglwys. Father was unable to add anything. He always felt a shortfall in knowledge about his heritage and often said as much. Both he and Mother were from the valleys of South Wales.

So, with the destination confirmed, Father explained things to Jessica and Daisy and showed them, with the help of details received from the USA, their own places within the larger family.

Then, he said a most important thing:

"You must remember that although we live in London and you were born here, the blood in your veins flows outwards from Wales and that's what counts."

He pointed to the letter and added, "Mind you, I can't even pronounce this last place that's mentioned. I'm hopeless at languages. It looks like 'Trefeg' followed by something or the other. I can take a stab at the first bit but who knows what the rest says?"

Mother smiled sympathetically. "It doesn't matter if you can say it; what counts is an opportunity to discover our roots. I'd like to learn more. Who knows what we'll find?"

Barry was listening, and he certainly liked the idea. He had never been outside London and found the prospect of visiting Wales very appealing. His general interest stemmed, as I've mentioned, from the fact that it is a land of legend, but he also had a specific reason for wanting to go. It concerned a story about a famous Welsh Spider called Llewellyn.

It was said that centuries ago Llewellyn had been able to spin a special web. When approached from one direction, it was as strong as steel because of the way the threads intertwined and crisscrossed; it could not be broken but could be passed through on command. Yet, when approached from the other direction, the thread was as sticky as the strongest glue and the unwitting victim would be entangled with no hope of escape.

Finally, and perhaps most interestingly, the web was completely invisible and inactive at Llewellyn's command.

For those of you with an interest in history, I might usefully add that Llewellyn was the second recorded Super Secret. He appeared a hundred and thirty years or so after Bonnie the Hidden became famous for the encouragement she offered Robert the Bruce in Scotland. Do not be surprised to learn that the first Super was female; in all creatures, their influence is, and always has been, the most important.

Anyway, I should return to the tale I am telling.

"Llewellyn the Web" had lived in the 1460s and spent most of his life in the land surrounding Harlech Castle before vanishing, probably across the Irish sea. The mystery of the web did not disappear with him but grew in the telling. So, Barry had his own reasons for visiting mid-Wales: he wanted to discover Llewellyn's secrets.

It is interesting to note that even at such a young age, with no idea or thought of what his future would hold, Barry felt a need to gather information and develop himself by gaining knowledge. In this matter, he was clearly wise beyond his years and set an example all creatures should follow.

Anyway, after days of stressful preparation, everything was squeezed into the car and off went Mother, Father, Jessica, Daisy and Barry.

The drive was uninteresting and, as always, I shall not waste precious time recounting unnecessary details. It was spent amidst the inevitable squabbles that occur when a people-family is squashed together for a few hours. It didn't bother Barry; he knew such things were normal. They followed the M4, crossed the Severn Bridge and turned right.

I do however need to tell you something else; there was another twist to the legend of Llewellyn's web.

It was said that before his thread could be spun once more, a message in the form of a riddle must be found and understood. A wall deep within Harlech Castle, not that far from a small village called Trefeglwys, was where the search should begin. Many had tried to find that beginning, but the web remained a mystery.

Do not think the riddle will be easy for you to untangle. To make matters even more difficult, the final words of a Spider riddle are always written elsewhere, and in this specific case, there will be another complication.

However, this is how it begins:

"What was once was only once was; so, to seek the secret of the web, you must find the intention written underneath and above and then you will………….."

It was a proper puzzle because it said what it said, but what did it say and not say? What was the intention underneath and above?

So, Barry had much on his mind as the car headed North. He was sure that if he could find the whole riddle he'd understand it.

To pass the time, and partly for his own amusement, he allowed the family to become lost. He could have ensured the correct roads were taken, but the trip was somewhat boring and there is humour in harmless error. It was a bit naughty in all honesty, but Barry was young, and all youth is undeveloped. Father also contributed to matters by insisting he knew the route. He also claimed that driving had been much more enjoyable when people used paper maps, without relying on satellite navigation!

"We are not going to use technology on this trip. There's far too much emphasis on it," he declared firmly. "People depend on buttons. I remember when you could simply wind the window down and ask for directions."

In the back of the car, Barry smiled and thought, *That's true, but prudence comes from progress, and it's a lesson well taught.* He liked to allow certain misconceptions to go unchecked, at least for a while.

The family had arranged bed and breakfast accommodation in a place called Llandanwg. It was thought to be an ideal spot for a general exploration of the area. They arrived later than intended, after an hour or two unintentionally spent exploring various country roads, but thankfully, the guest house was perfect. The family had a fish and chips supper and went to bed. When all was quiet, Barry began his investigation.

There was a medieval church nearby. It was prime territory to find the contacts who could provide some necessary information.

The best place to find most Spiders is usually outside. Barry looked thoughtfully at the tombstones before searching for locals and asking them the obvious question.

"I'm trying to find out more about the legend of Llewellyn. Can you help?"

It took all night, but eventually, he gained an encouraging response. After many hours of being met with stony silence, it marked a beginning.

"Why should Llewellyn interest you?"

"Because I wish to learn the secret of the web," Barry answered.

He had decided honesty was the best policy – it usually is.

"Is that right?" said the local. "Well, it's not a secret that can be told, so if I were you, I'd be on my way."

"No, listen, you don't understand," said Barry who explained, as best he could, his reasons for trying to find things out. It was difficult to do because he didn't fully know what they were. All he knew was that he would be able to use the answer to the riddle wisely and usefully. So he just rambled on for a while. In fact, some of the words coming out of his mouth didn't feel, or sound, like he was saying them. Sometimes, we all speak without thinking as if the words come from elsewhere.

"I'm none the wiser after that," the local mumbled. "It sounded good though. Hang about, I'll go and find Grumpy Owen."

He disappeared before reappearing with another Spider.

Barry was intrigued.

"Why do they call you Grumpy?" he inquired politely.

"What's it got to do with you?" came the reply.

It was perhaps not the best of starts, but it got better. Grumpy was a Spider who had studied The Chronicles and knew about Llewellyn's web.

He listened with growing interest before asking a few questions. In answering, Barry had again been unable to recognise his own voice.

This is really peculiar, he thought. *Who on earth is saying this?*

Anyway, Grumpy didn't seem bothered about such vocal origins. He went to talk with some others who also came over to ask even more questions.

Eventually, they huddled together and spoke in a language they assumed Barry wouldn't understand, but of course, he did. He couldn't hear every word but the bits he could make out were confusing. It appeared he was expected.

Grumpy spoke again.

"You need to go to Harlech Castle tonight. It will be a half-moon. Find Branwen. She's a descendent of Llewellyn and will consider what you say."

"How will I know her?" asked Barry.

"She'll know you."

It was the end of the conversation.

Meanwhile, the family had woken up bright and breezy and were considering what to do with their day.

"Please, may we go to the beach and paddle in the sea?" asked Daisy.

"It's not exactly sunny, is it?" Jessica muttered sarcastically.

It was, in truth, a typical Welsh day – wet. The rain was pouring down.

Mother looked out of the window and said, "I can see why Wales is called the land of plenty; there's plenty of rain. Never mind though, there are lots of things to do. I've been reading some tourist brochures. Why don't we drive over to Talgarth Manor this morning? It looks really interesting, with a history dating back to the 12th century. Alternatively, we could go to Gregynog Hall; all the references there are about the Davies sisters. Perhaps they're something to do with Dad! We can go to the beach afterwards if the weather improves."

"Oh joy," muttered Jessica, receiving a scowl from Mother in return. Daisy looked disappointed but said nothing.

"It's supposed to brighten up later," Mother said with an encouraging smile to her youngest daughter.

The family had booked the bed and breakfast place for the weekend, so with their luggage safely unpacked, there was a lot more room in the car as they drove towards Talgarth.

Barry had returned but didn't go with them. He wanted to be fully prepared and ready to meet Branwen. After resting a while to collect his thoughts, he returned to the church grounds to confirm what he had already seen; somehow he knew it was important.

The day was mostly done before he was satisfied, so he went straight to Harlech and prepared to meet Branwen.

The castle itself was really a most impressive place, cold and foreboding as the night gradually descended. Historic events involving Llewellyn could readily be imagined, even though they happened nearly 600 years ago.

They were different times for sure, thought Barry as he waited for his moment.

Instinct is often the guide to illumination, and after a few hours he suddenly announced, "I'm here to find what cannot be seen."

Barry had excellent night vision but eyesight was not guiding his actions.

A voice replied.

"We have long guarded this place and the knowledge inside, so why do you think that is something we will allow?"

"Because it is time for the telling," said Barry. "Branwen is expecting me."

"What would you say to what was once was only once was?" asked the voice.

"Nothing of that to you. Take me to her."

It was a sensible reply and Barry waited in the following silence.

The night was still; the rain had stopped.

He had realised there might be some preliminaries to get through, but prolonged inactivity didn't suit the mood he was now in. He lost patience and walked towards where he knew Branwen would be. After using web thread to descend a flight of steps into the dungeon, he looked around.

No Spiders tried to bar his path, but he felt their presence.

He saw the smallest of openings leading further downwards below the flagstones. Squeezing through, he entered a space where very few creatures had ever been and eagerly studied the markings on the walls.

"This isn't what might be called luxury accommodation," he said.

Branwen answered, "I know of little difference between a place and a palace, and I live in neither. Why look at the walls for scratchings that by themselves explain nothing?"

She had a voice unlike any other. It contained a Welsh lilt that instantly aroused interest and commanded attention. All who heard her speak could remember every word and wanted more said. Voices were always important to Barry. The differences in each intrigued him and are, in fact, very interesting. Many stories can be told about sound.

Barry explained, "I am here for a beginning and an end. There are things I want to know, and only you can speak of them."

"Why do you say so?"

"Because of Llewellyn."

"What do you know of Llewellyn?"

"What I have seen and heard."

Branwen studied Barry.

"Llewellyn caused something of you to be written in The Chronicles. It is why you have reached this place."

It was an unexpected remark.

"That doesn't make sense. I'm not mentioned in The Chronicles. How could Llewellyn know of me? Where am I mentioned?" Barry questioned.

He thought he saw a smile, but it left as quickly as it came.

"You are not mentioned, but in a Revelation, there is enough."

So, in the gloomy, coal-black space of the deepest depth within Harlech Castle on one Saturday evening, perhaps the greatest of the Spider mysteries was at last spoken of in order to help explain what once was.

Part 2

Branwen began slowly, "It was a time when fingers were toes. This castle was besieged by the many; the few had nothing. Yet, it sustained the longest known siege ever recorded in these islands. How could it happen? Through seven years, the impossible existed but the impossible cannot exist, so what took place? Look through all the books that people write, and little is written. No one knows how Llewellyn kept this castle safe. The way it happened was never seen and has never been repeated. Harlech Castle stands unique because what cannot be explained remains silent and the books stay empty. Only a song speaks of it."

"Men of Harlech," said Barry.

She smiled. "In Wales, we know music is the best of tokens."

Barry listened with rapt attention as Branwen continued; her voice hypnotic.

"Llewellyn spun a web around the castle. Those starting from within could pass and return at their leisure, but those outside could not enter and, on trying, would stick fast together. The web was invisible and so the rumours began. Since then, many have wanted to know more."

"Then I am one of many."

"You think it and may even wish it, but it is not so and why should it be?" Branwen answered.

She smiled. "There will be times when, seeking knowledge, you fail to understand. Why search for something by looking time and time again in the same barren place? Better to quickly learn what is not there to find. You have no need of Llewellyn's web, only a need for the learning it brings. That is the beginning you seek."

As she continued, Barry realised he was hearing guidance from The Chronicles.

"So listen to me carefully. What you want is not what is wanted. A moment gone can never return. History contains a promise, nothing more; it is not to be relied upon. You are in Harlech asking for answers, but here Llewellyn must rule."

Branwen continued to talk, using words I cannot repeat. Only one part remains to be told, and that will come later. Many times, what passes between Spiders is not for me to say.

I can, however, disclose Chapter 8, Paragraph 11, of The Chronicles as the short passage to which Branwen had referred. It was regarded as being very useful to those seeking information.

> *"Do not linger when it is time to progress. Realise that it is not for you to know everything. Curiosity must disappear or become harmful, not helpful as intended, and one must learn this lesson or fail themselves and be sorry."*

Branwen left and the rain started. Barry stayed and stared at the walls. He had much to consider and took in all he could. His life would forever be different.

At breakfast on Sunday, the family was talking about the previous day. Barry was there to ensure everything was in order.

"I've never seen so many sheep!" said Father. "They completely blocked the road."

Mother laughed. "We did the right thing by turning around and heading in the other direction. I just couldn't wait any longer. No one even tried to clear the way. Perhaps that's how it is in Wales; sheep have priority."

The family laughed.

Even Barry grinned. *True*, he thought.

It was a good start to their day but, as Mother reminded everyone, they were also in Wales to try and learn more about their family roots.

"That's so boring though," lamented Jessica.

Mother was firm.

"Stop complaining. It's very important to know where you're from if you want to know where you're going. It's one of the reasons we came here."

"I just don't see how great grandfathers and the like can possibly make any difference in my life," replied Jessica, "but if it makes you happy, then don't mind me."

Mother glared at her.

"You can't live in the past, but you can learn from it. Being Welsh has always made me and your Father proud; it means a lot to us. Try and understand."

Giving up on Jessica for the moment, she turned hopefully to Daisy.

"What about you? Wouldn't you like to know more about our long-lost relatives?"

"I suppose so, but I would also like to go to the beach, play in the rocks and paddle in the sea," she answered.

"Of course. Let's do it!" Father laughed. "The sun is due to shine later this morning, and we can't miss that chance! This trip is not just about me, you know. I want all of us to be happy."

"Are you sure?" asked Mother sympathetically.

He nodded. "We can check out Trefegowhatsit on the way home tomorrow."

The landlady was busy bringing tea, toast and a variety of jams to the table, but she stopped to stare curiously at Father.

"Excuse me, it's been on my mind – do I know you from somewhere?" she asked.

"I shouldn't think so. We live in London, although my ancestors were from these parts," he replied proudly.

"Oh, that's lovely!" She beamed and looked thoughtful. "Well, don't mind me saying, but if you've got some spare time, take a drive to Llandanwg Hall. It's not too far if you can find it, and it's open to the public on Sundays. I'm sure you'd find it interesting."

After spending an hour or two at the seaside waiting for the rain to stop, it was clear that the landlady's comments had left an impression on Mother. She was intrigued.

"Let's quickly go to that place the landlady suggested, whatever it's called – Llandanniwig or something. We can come back here later."

The road signs seemed to show the way, so they set off. Barry went with them, but no matter how much Father tried, he simply could not get there. After a few hours, he'd had enough. Barry did nothing to help.

"Right. It's happening again. This is hopeless. We keep going in circles and returning to the same place. It's like some sort of grand Welsh conspiracy. Don't they have any proper signposts? Let's forget all about Llandiggywiggy Hall. I've never heard of it before anyway. I don't care what the landlady said. Let's just go somewhere findable. Where do you fancy?"

Mother agreed. She was fed up with life without satellite navigation.

"I know we talked about the beach but who'd like a ride on a train up a big mountain?" she asked cheerily.

"Yes, please," voiced Daisy. "Then the beach!"

"I suppose that's a bit different," offered Jessica.

The family promptly headed for Snowdonia and, for the rest of the day, thoroughly enjoyed themselves without mishap or other incidents relevant to this story.

Barry stayed in the car enjoying the wonderful scenery and resting. It had been a busy time, and he was glad of the chance to relax.

Soon, it was time to leave Wales, and as Mother and Father had agreed, on the way back to London, they would try and find out something about their family roots. After all, Trefeglwys was practically on their way.

On that Monday morning, Barry made sure they got there without difficulty. There were still some loose threads to tie up.

Branwen had said something else in relation to the Davies family's connections, and I promised to tell you a little more of it.

"Do you see this?" she had asked Barry, pointing to the riddle that was still as clearly visible as when it was first placed on the wall.

"What do you imagine it means?" she asked.

Barry voiced what he saw, slowly and surely.

"What was once was only once was," he began. He read it all carefully and turned the possibilities over in his head. "I keep thinking that the word 'was' is important. I can't get past it. It's used three times, right at the start. It must be significant."

Branwen smiled. "You are right, but although a visual impression is all very well it's nothing without the rewards. What use to begin without understanding the ending?"

She continued, "I can tell you that for over 600 years, no one destined to confirm the secret of the web has stood here."

There was a long pause as if Branwen was remembering past events. Barry stayed respectfully silent, imagining Llewellyn in Harlech castle.

Eventually, Branwen spoke again.

"Many have sought to complete the riddle, but it is not so simple. Remember, you will be unable to understand something that requires no understanding. I suggest you stay here and reflect on what is found and what need not be sought."

"I'm sorry, but that's too unclear. Please, what did Llewellyn mean?" asked Barry.

"Simply that the web is not to be made available in future times – not to you nor anyone. It was for a moment that shall not come again, but the secret of the web is different. You can arrive with nothing but leave with much if you learn from the past yet live in the present. We need say no more on that to each other, but before you go, I must tell you something about the father in your people-family."

Later, Barry would think of the situation Llewellyn had faced all those years ago as a Super Spider. The responsibility of trying to find a solution to the problem of conflict between those in the castle and those outside would have weighed heavily on his shoulders. Conversation yielded no answers, so something else was needed. Whatever it was would surely be useful many times over, judging by the ways in which people still foolishly conduct themselves.

However, he knew his thoughts needed to be applied against the wording of the riddle and placed within The Chronicles. He had also heard more about the family connection that Father was seeking and it was causing him concern.

To call Trefeglwys a busy village would be a vast overstatement. There was a pub, which was closed, and some houses dotted along the main street; a school overlooked everything from the vantage point of a hillside and, as always, a church dominated the scene. It had parking spaces outside and that was where Father left the car. Barry stayed behind; he had no need to do anything.

Father entered the church grounds through a rusty gate. Spiders were watching him closely, but he was unaware of them. There were rows and rows of tombstones bearing the inscription of one Davies or another. Surely, these were relatives – at least one of them anyway? Yet, he knew it wasn't necessarily true and gave it little thought.

He wandered up and down, trying to read the faded epitaphs and inscriptions; there were many indicating a short and hard life.

"Poor things," he said softly.

With the family still waiting in the car, Father exited through another gate and wandered along the main street.

At the last house on the left, an old man was pottering in the garden.

"Excuse me," said Father, but the man didn't respond.

Father tried again, and this time he was heard. The old man put down his shovel and came forward to where Father was waiting.

"Ah, we're from London, but it seems my family lived here some 150 years ago, or more. Our name is Davies. I have a letter from relatives in the US pointing me to this place. I'm looking to find out what I can."

"Nice to meet you. I'm Tudor," came the response. "Davies, eh? Well, there are plenty of them around here."

"Indeed." Father smiled. "I was hoping there might be some local historian or something; someone I could talk to."

He spoke rather loudly after realising Tudor was a trifle deaf. He wished he'd prepared things better instead of just turning up and expecting something good to happen. There is an old saying which goes, "Fail to prepare and prepare to fail". It is relevant to this story and was most certainly one of the prudent lessons Barry had wanted Father to learn.

"Can I see the letter?" asked Tudor, sensing the air of disappointment.

"Yes, of course," replied Father, handing it over.

The old man read it, or at least the first part of it, and told Father something Barry already knew.

"This is the wrong Trefeglwys."

Perhaps I might usefully interrupt this story to say that the word, when properly pronounced, sounds something like "Tref-fig-go-weis".

Anyway, let's continue with what Tudor was saying.

"The letter shows the address as being in Cardiganshire, but this is Montgomeryshire, so you're in a different place! Mind you, you'll probably still have relatives somewhere down there."

He pointed to the graveyard and winked knowingly.

"Bound to have," he added.

Father looked very sad; he couldn't hide his feelings. Yet, upon looking more closely at the letter, he could see the old man was right. Why on earth couldn't he have been more careful? He felt really stupid!

Tudor was sympathetic.

"It's a mistake easily made. The name means township with a church, and there's a lot of them. You obviously thought one Trefeglwys was as good as another."

With that, he went back to his gardening.

Father returned to the car where the family was waiting.

"I'm an idiot," he said sheepishly.

"Why? What happened?" asked Mother.

"It turns out there's more than one Trefigowisis, and we're in the wrong one!"

Mother could see Father was upset. "Oh, is that how you say it? Never mind. How far away are we from the right one?"

"Oh no," said Father. "I'm not even sure, and I can't ask everyone to go through all this again. We're on our way back to London. I've lived this long without knowing about my family's past, and I'm sure I can go on perfectly well without the details."

"I don't mind if we go to the other place," Jessica said kindly.

"Nor me," added Daisy.

Their reaction reminded Father that something better than disappointment is always worth finding.

"That's really sweet, but not all history is so important. What we have here and now is what counts. We're together as a family. Come on, let's just go home. After all, there could be more Trefiggyos dotted about."

It did sound like a much better idea, so that was what they did; it was time to move on.

A few miles away, at Llandanwg Hall, a visitor would have seen a painting hanging on the wall in the dining room. It showed William Herbert, sometimes known as "Black William" because of his cruel streak and unhappy disposition. He commanded the forces outside Harlech Castle during the siege. His loyalty to King Edward meant he owned large areas of Welsh land. Over time, many of his children – he had at least 10 – had married locally, and the name Davies was acquired and spread.

The landlady had noticed the likeness of Father to William.

Barry had carefully considered what his people-family should know. It was not an easy decision, but he decided to leave matters as they stood; circumstances dictate events. It was best to concentrate on the big picture. He had needed to learn about Llewellyn's web, which meant visiting Harlech Castle, and there was an obvious Trefeglwys nearby. He had been listening when Father had described the family tree to Daisy and Jessica; connections are everywhere.

During the journey back to London, Barry became increasingly comfortable with the events of the past few days. He had completed the riddle and understood why the past must be left behind in order to make the most of the present. Branwen had explained that the Davies family roots should actually be traced to Llanbadarn Trefeglwys, near the coast and about 50 miles away. The letter from America was somewhat incomplete and not of any relevance. She said a family was presented with opportunities, nothing more.

The web was a creation of the moment; it was not available on demand. When you consider every word of the riddle you might begin to understand, and if you had seen and heard the events of 1465 it would be clear why it was written.

So do not allow curiosity to become harmful when there are greater things to notice.

Yet there is still more to say.

Llewellyn caused the riddle to be completed in 3 places, one for each of the words concerned.

It was above a name on the oldest tombstone in the graveyard near to where Grumpy Owen lived, and below the same name on a tombstone at the church in Trefeglwys.

Father had seen the name, but the riddle was completed in Welsh and so he passed it by with barely a glance.

The third location was somewhere near Aberystwyth and isn't relevant to this story.

The ending of the riddle had also become a family motto, displayed on a framed portrait of William Herbert, 1st Earl of Pembroke.

The secret of the web remains a mystery to those who cannot find it; the web itself was gone forever.

03

Barry Explains Spyderisms

"It's a different direction
So maybe I won't go there today
It feels too strange,
Yet I've thought of it often
How would it look from somewhere new
But I'm scared of change.
And I've got my past
Dragging me down
It's hard to let go for me
Because the time never arrives
It travels too slow for me,
So what do I say to the voice in the night
As it slip-streams along?
It's making me weak
It's not making me strong."

Part 1

What do you notice about the following paragraph? Everything within it is a Spyderism, a coded means of communication I shall describe in more detail a little later. It contains only two sentences, but study them and see if you can notice any peculiarities before further explanations. The story itself begins at paragraph 3.

"Reservoir swimmers, gaining momentum, accidentally taught skinny dippers river skills. Afterwoods teenage onlookers, opposite tree root stumps, freely donated classic green grass, growing 2 yellow colourless territorial weeds."

The day started like any other. I suppose most days have much the same beginning but then events happen, and some have hidden and significant consequences. For instance, think about the many times you have picked something up and then dropped it. No gain or loss seems to have arisen if it is quickly retrieved so what was the purpose of it being dropped? Yet, it happened for a reason, or did it?

This tale illustrates how the most important acts can take different forms and are not always a matter of chance or choice, but sometimes a matter of interpretation. Therefore, the language by which communication takes place is really important and is why Spyderism needs to be explained.

Barry was on his morning walk. For some reason, he decided to go further than usual and passed by the roundabout marking the southern boundary of Louvain Terrace.

He was moving through the gardens of Curre Street when he saw a Spider called Hannah. She waved a leg to beckon him over.

"What a surprise! We don't often see you in these parts, Barry, but I'm glad you're here because I have a question for you," she said.

"Sure. What is it?" he replied.

Before going any further, I should explain that in the world of Spiders, there are many superstitions, myths and notions. From time to time, they resurface and everyone becomes engrossed in a discussion about the rights, wrongs, relevance and, indeed, even the likelihood of the particular subject in focus.

It was such a time. The issue was concerned with how a life is shaped and how it has nothing to do with where or when you were born but everything to do with the name by which you become known.

This may not seem like much to get excited about, but Spiders invest a great deal of significance in the way they are individually referenced. They believe words are important, as we see from another story I have told in this book, and because words consist of letters it must mean letters are important. The way they are brought together and interact describes everything, so they are capable of many meanings.

Incidentally, numbers are also important, and perhaps, in time, you will hear more about their particular intricacies. As a small example, I know of a family that owned 4 houses numbered 8, 17, 44 and 116. No thought was given to a connection, but it is there for all to see. At another level, consider that in an election, you may have a million supporters but if the opposing side has one million and one, then all sorts of consequences become possible based on a solitary extra number but whose vote was it? Think about how – and when – one becomes more influential than a million, and you will see why numbers can produce outcomes that letters cannot. Carefully contemplate the following phrase used by Secrets, "one in a million and one in one million and one in a million and one".

In any event, both letters and numbers are the bedrock on which the world turns, and it is a mistake to take them for granted. Spyderism acknowledges the importance of both, but in this story, I shall concentrate on letters and explain how they can both mislead and instruct. Most importantly, Spyderism reveals more than you need to know, but never less than is needed, by keeping simplicity from the complex.

In Spider society, every possible letter permutation has supporters. Some feel the available evidence confirms that if a name has the same letter within it, side by side, it indicates a strong, favoured and fortunate individual; many Secrets have this "double". At the other end of the scale is a name with the same letter at the start and end. Such Spiders can be "difficult" because it is thought highly undesirable to finish in the same place as where you started. Between those extremes are words with letters that mirror and face each other to provide peace and symmetry, like "lapdog".

Every variation has a faithful following. One faction even practises the non-inclusion of letters or even a word. Sometimes, the omissions might be something obvious and unarguable, but at other times there are different interpretations of what was meant. Single letters and numbers can appear in sentences when circumstances permit, and commas and full stops are obviously allowed because of the "double". An unbreakable rule, which I follow, is that for many words, including Spiders,

Secret Spiders and Spyderisms, a capital letter must always be used.

So, Hannah clearly had much to consider, and her question went straight to the heart of the matter.

"What is your view on letters, Barry? I'm really confused. Does the way by which we are known prove very much?"

You may wonder why she asked Barry for his opinion.

It was because a very few chosen Spiders inherit a rich store of wisdom and knowledge accumulated by others over many centuries. It passes onto them naturally and easily and gives them great influence over their community. Although he was still very young, everyone who met Barry could see that he might be "chosen", which meant his views were always of the greatest possible interest.

This responsibility made it important for him to answer every question very carefully.

"Names do matter, Hannah, but they aren't decisive," he said after a moment of reflection. "Various things happen in a lifetime because everything in the world is out there somewhere. The way you begin certainly offers a range of openings, but then it is for the individual to proceed. It is your own decision or indecision that forms the next connection."

Hannah wasn't sure she understood what Barry meant by "the next connection" and was not even convinced she wanted to know. She felt, quite correctly, that some things were better and made more sense when not understood. Unfortunately, it also meant she often heard what she wanted to be said.

"It's just very confusing. My name has always caused me problems."

It was all she could think of saying by way of explanation; it was an emotional subject.

As always, Barry wanted to be helpful.

"A name only offers options, Hannah. The individual must select which to follow. It's true that other names would not have provided the same opportunities, but it is you who possess and control the future, not your name."

He saw the troubled look on her face and wondered how best to put her mind at ease. It wasn't easy and Barry began to feel the kind of frustration you get when wanting to help but unable to do so.

He tried again.

"Look, a name is just a reference point. In a sense, many words and names have interesting parallel formations or sounds without any special, individual significance. Put letters and words together and something meaningful can come about, but in isolation they often mean nothing. The truth is that we receive a beginning but write our own ending. Don't believe in being helpless; it is for the individual to find happiness or sadness when both are available."

Barry felt on safe ground with this answer because he was quoting The Chronicles from which all the wisdom in Spider Land derives. Their guidance on the matter was found in Chapter 10, paragraph 3:

"The unwise fail to realise how everything must be unfinished because what is presented is a mere beginning to be completed. It is clear that the more you age, the older you become and greater wisdom and change is then available; yet still, you will never know much more than nothing. Many things can happen in a lifetime but, although only some come about, each was started in a moment gone by for you to decide how, or if, they progress."

This information had clearly been lost on Hannah. It is remarkable how all creatures are able to ignore the best advice. However, The Chronicles are the essential foundation in the evolution of every Spider, and the above paragraph certainly deserved her better attention.

Incidentally, The Chronicles were begun long before Spyderisms were recognised. Their purpose has always been to prepare Spiders for a changing future by helping them react wisely to choices and new information. As with all such books, this type of objective creates a position for specialist instructors who claim an ability, sometimes falsely, to interpret the teachings. In Spider society the role is undertaken by "Secrets", and offers some flexibility in that such Spiders need not necessarily conform to the major Spyderism naming conventions. For instance, in due course, Barry would meet Derek, whose doubled letter was "one-in" from the start and end of his name.

Two more things should be noted in passing. Firstly, the Secrets who interpret The Chronicles for the benefit of others must be judged worthy of doing so by virtue of the wisdom they provide. Secondly, The Chronicles react to developments in the world by revealing "missing" paragraphs never seen before because they were not previously needed. This new guidance is initially shown to a selected Secret in order that, when correctly understood, it can be widely communicated. Until then the words concerned are underlined. It is how The Chronicles update and remain relevant, but to learn more about them and the significance of Revelations you must read elsewhere.

Hannah was still looking miserable.

"I have a friend called Phillip," she said. "He didn't like his life. I remember him saying he needed to completely change it around. He talked about 'Day One' and 'One Day'."

"I understand that," Barry nodded. "By delaying change until tomorrow, it was 'One Day', but it becomes 'Day One' from the time of the change. It's why succeeded lasts longer than success, although both are interesting concepts. The better truth is that you are successful when you think it and are what you are when you know it."

Actually, this was a particularly revealing insight from Barry because the meaning would later play a significant part in an important Revelation he would receive in order to confirm his own status.

His mind flashed back to Spider school, where the ways by which all things are connected formed a big part in explaining the other lessons. The teacher had discussed the meaning of letters as a very specific part of the curriculum.

The teaching was as follows:

"Spiders and people are often in close proximity, and so each can learn from the other. We think about and recognise the meaning of letters, but people are far less aware of their importance. Yet, ask them to name their favourite painter, and many would say Picasso; ask who was the greatest Englishman and they would probably say Churchill, although for several reasons some argue it to be Newton. Time will show that the most important scientist was Chargaff and the most influential musician, Beethoven. The greatest philosophers were Rousseau and Wittgenstein.

"The strongest animal is a gorilla, the fastest a cheetah. The wisest bird is not an owl but a cuckoo or maybe a parrot. The best workers are not ants but bees and it is our special insight, as given by The Chronicles, that makes us Spiders. Green is the most promised colour in nature. Valleys, butterflies, seeds, sunsets – so it goes on. Food, feeling and communication sustain life, and the greatest place is always the seat of learning, a school, where books are used.

"The way in which events come together through letters is also overlooked. Our biggest game is Stones, whereas for people, it is football, and their favoured team is Liverpool. From that city came The Beetles, although to confuse matters the Coloured Spiders caused a misspelling. How many have noticed that all four members had doubled adjacent letters? One even needed to change his name to include a double before joining. So, you can see how combinations and numbers come together to achieve great results. Sometimes, the attraction is more obvious than at other times; nonetheless, it always exists. History teaches that a king can never have the importance or influence of a queen,

letters will overcome numbers and accuracy must eventually triumph over suspicion."

Barry had always kept this lesson in mind, although unconvinced that a few random shapes could mean very much. Remember that he operated at a higher level of understanding and, in keeping with the teachings of The Chronicles, knew all about misinterpretation.

"Listen, Hannah. You may think, or have been told, that life must be perfect but it isn't true. You will never know everything, and there is no need. The very best things you see or hear are always unfinished, even if they seem complete. They may not appear so, but that is how they best convey their meaning when presented. It is a big mistake to expect completion; simply try to make progress and accept what is before you. Appearances are there for a reason, and all teaching is conducted in languages that are, and remain, imperfect until they can adequately describe love and pain, not sorrow."

They separated, but the conversation stayed in Barry's mind; there was something more he should have said but wasn't sure what it was. He realised that Phillip didn't exist, Hannah was referring to herself.

A few days later, the postman came to Louvain Terrace. Barry always looked out for the red van driving along the road. He liked the promise of something about to arrive and how "letters" were sent to "numbers".

However, this morning, Barry noticed the mail on the mat was for number 12, though he and his people-family lived at number 14. It was addressed to Mr S. N. Babb.

Barry didn't know much about his neighbour, but everything is connected, so he resolved to find out more. After the conversation with Hannah, it was a coincidence too strong to ignore.

The most obvious starting point for more information would be with a resident at number 12 who would know a lot about the character of the people-family they lived with.

Fortunately, Barry was on good terms with the Spiders on that side of the terrace, unlike with Roger at number 16. Among the options, he thought Frank would be the best source of information. He had been living next door for a long time and was good friends with Sinbad – one of the garden Spiders at number 14.

Barry popped through the fence later that morning.

"Babs is as good as gold, Barry," Frank reported. "He treats us well – very considerate. For instance, at painting and decorating time, he moves us gently out of the way. It's the same with everyone. He's a great guy with a sunny disposition. We're all treated like a part of the family. In fact, 'Babs, your uncle' is a joke amongst us."

Barry grinned. He thought it funny that Mr Babb was known as Babs by the residents, but he wasn't totally satisfied with the other information. He sensed there was more to discover. Yet, Frank wouldn't say a bad word about Babs.

Arriving back home, his mind returned to Hannah and the meaning of names and the opportunities they provided. The way their meeting had ended wasn't to his liking; he needed to do more.

He decided to go and see her again but the trouble was, no matter where he looked, she couldn't be found.

Eventually, he asked the local ants. They went everywhere, and if someone needed to be located, it was usually best to ask them.

The local commander asked, "Why do you want to find her?"

Barry felt no need to be secretive; he appreciated curiosity.

"She came to me for advice, and I wasn't of much use. I feel a special duty to help others, and it bothers me when I don't."

The ant was puzzled.

"I've never understood why Spiders like you are prepared to spend so much time on the weak and needy. If only you concentrated on important matters, then there might be some real improvements in the world. The way I look at it is very simple: those that are strong can prosper and the rest mustn't be allowed to spoil things."

"That's a terrible attitude, and I hope no Spider would ever adopt it," replied Barry frowning. "I certainly look at things differently. No one is actually weak or needy, it's just that they haven't travelled far on their journey. Some of those you would discard have eventually been responsible for great ideas and developments. Being able to take someone a little further along is a special gift."

"Let's not argue, Barry; it doesn't change anything. Ants and Spiders are different. Let's leave it at that. I'm sure you'll find her, but it has nothing to do with us."

It was a disappointing response. Days went by. It would have been easy to forget about Hannah, but that wasn't Barry's way. He became increasingly curious about Mr Babb and somehow felt the misdelivered letter indicated a connection with Hannah. What could it be?

This feeling caused Barry to stay on high alert as far as next door was concerned, and he kept a close eye on all the comings and goings. During the day, everything seemed normal, so he extended his observations into the late evening. It wasn't long before, under the moonlight, he saw Babs burying a box in the garden.

Barry knew people did strange things, but this was really unusual. What was inside?

The mystery intensified when, the next evening, Barry saw Babs dig the box up.

Why would someone bury anything only to recover it 24 hours later?

Part 2

The next approach Barry tried in his search for Hannah was talking to Tombstone, the family dog at number 12. He spent the most time with Babs, and although Barry was far from confident he'd get anything useful from him, he thought he would try.

Barry was well acquainted with Tombstone. They had first crossed paths because of the dog's unwelcome habit of wandering into the garden at number 14 and digging up the flower beds. Indeed, there was a time when Barry thought he should put a stop to it, but he knew animals must be allowed to be as they are and not as you want them. So instead, he planted thoughts in the heads of Mother and Father that such minor intrusions were nothing to be overly upset about.

He found Tombstone lying on the grass chewing a stick.

"Hi, Tom. Can I please have a word with you about your master?" asked Barry.

Tombstone looked up.

"Fine," he said gruffly, clearly unhappy at being disturbed.

"I saw you in the garden when Babs buried a box, which he then dug up the next night. You're a great one for digging, so what's going on? There must have been something inside. What was it?"

"Beats me. I just do as I'm told around here," said Tombstone. "Dogs don't go into much detail. He brought a box home after one of our park walks. He got it from his brother's house. It didn't matter to me that he promptly buried it. I did think about digging it up later, but there wasn't time."

"Is there anything of interest about the box you can tell me?" asked Barry.

"Not really. All I know is that it takes too long to get to the park because Babs stops and talks to people on the way. Everyone seems to want a word with him, and I'm told to just wait quietly."

So, as expected, not much was to be gained from talking to a dog. They are the most loyal of creatures but have little to offer beyond companionship and some limited training possibilities. They operate solely on the basis that they need to be accountable which, as we shall see, is an admirable quality and very different from the way cats look at things. Actually, the distinguishing features between cats and dogs would soon become more important in Barry's life.

Still, Barry had noted something of interest, Curre Street was on the way to Victoria Park.

He resolved to find the box, which was presumably somewhere inside number 12. It must contain something of interest, and he needed to find out what it was.

The house layout was basically the same as number 14 and so was easy to explore, but no matter where he searched, there was no sign of the box. Barry concluded it was no longer on the premises.

The next thing that happened was Hannah's reappearance.

"What's going on, Hannah?" asked Barry. "I couldn't find you for days, and then here you are in Louvain Terrace. I wanted to say something more about letters. I've been a bit distracted lately on something else, but I haven't forgotten."

"I've moved in next door. There was a vacancy and here I am," she said, beaming. "That's what I've come to tell you. It's made such a difference. The place in Curre Street became too uncomfortable. The main problem was the owner. Such a miserable man. He was dragging all of us down with his mood swings, and he hated Spiders. I already knew you lived in Louvain Terrace and thought it must be a good spot. Then, I found out more about Babs. He has a reputation for being kind and thoughtful, so I was happy to move in. I've found a nice little corner, and it's much better for me than Curre Street."

"You'd heard of Babs already then?" asked Barry, who was still intent on learning what he could.

"Yes, a bit. He often used to call in and chat with his brother; they have such different personalities. It was obvious he was much nicer than Silas."

"Silas?" queried Barry. "Who's Silas?"

"That's his brother – the householder in Curre Street. Funny sort of man. He used to be okay, but he changed a lot when his parents died, and then the whole house and garden became too uncomfortable. So, with one thing and another, I decided to move," answered Hannah. "I tried somewhere else, but that didn't work out. This is the right place for me."

"Hang on a minute," Barry said. "Silas lives here in Louvain Terrace; he's Babs."

"Ha, so you don't know everything. David is the one living here; he's Babs. Silas lives in Curre Street."

Hannah confirmed the information with a big smile, clearly pleased she could tell Barry something he didn't know. Barry had never seen her look so happy.

It was a complicated picture.

It had started with Hannah asking about the meaning of letters. Then, the man next door buried a box and dug it up again. His brother lived in the house that Hannah had lived in before she moved to Louvain Terrace. Each brother seemed very different. A letter meant for one address was delivered to another, and so there clearly was scope for confusion over names.

"Tell me, Hannah," Barry said, "what's the layout of the house in Curre Street? I have to go there, and it'd be helpful to have some sort of idea what to expect."

"Really?" Hannah was surprised. "Well, it's straightforward enough; they're not big houses. There's a small entrance corridor from the street with a room for entertaining on the left. Follow along into the main room, where people generally are, and beyond that is the kitchen and bathroom. The stairs are accessed from the main room. There are three bedrooms, all of different sizes: the biggest, where Silas sleeps, another bedroom and then one that is really no more than a little box room, where I used to live. Why are you going there?"

Barry ignored the question.

"You haven't mentioned anyone except Silas. Does he live alone?"

"Yes, he does now," she said. "If you're going to Curre Street, I'm coming too."

Barry didn't argue.

There was no need to waste time so, that evening, they made their way there using web thread and arrived, as it happened, just before David and Tombstone.

Barry had undertaken a quick exploration and found nothing obvious. So he settled down behind the sofa as the brothers began talking, making sure the dog couldn't tell he and Hannah were in the room. Something of interest might be said, and now that he knew the layout he could have a more thorough search for the box anytime.

"I'm sorry, Norman. I was wrong to take it away, but at least I soon brought it back," said David. "You should keep it."

"Norman? Who's Norman?" Barry whispered to Hannah.

"It's the same one as Silas," she whispered back.

Barry poked his head out a little further and, for the first time, saw both brothers together.

They did look very alike.

David was still speaking. "My conscience quickly got the better of me. I had actually buried the box in the garden before the extent and implications of my mistake became obvious when I read the letter meant for you. Letters follow numbers, eh? No, I see now that it's only right, everything stays here."

"It's not a problem," said Norman, who was clearly relaxed about the whole situation. "I was confident you'd return the box, and that's what matters. Funny how, as time passes, we realise what was always hidden in plain sight. It's actually fortunate that the last of the letters was sent to the wrong address."

The conversation carried on but nothing else said in Curre Street that night is of any relevance to this tale, so need not be recounted. I've said it before but vast volumes of words as expressed and written are completely useless. Countless passages can be passed over with no detriment to the story. Too much detail causes a message to be lost, and Spyderisms highlight the unnecessary around the important.

Barry and Hannah returned to Louvain Terrace. She was none the wiser, but Barry had understood a couple of new things.

Most importantly was something Barry could use to help Hannah; within his family, Silas was known by his middle name.

He said to her, "Come and see me the day after tomorrow. Silas and David may be brothers, but they are very different, and I think I know why."

On the appointed day, Hannah found Barry in his house under the kitchen sink at number 14. He was surrounded by various pieces of paper.

"What's all this?" she asked, pointing a leg.

Barry replied, "I went back to Curre Street and found the box. It helped me prepare for this talk. You remember asking about the meaning of letters? Well, I was thinking about how best to show why that is not the most critical thing because most letters are mere accessories along the path to meaning. Only a few words are key, as these will explain."

He pointed to the pieces of paper.

Hannah looked puzzled.

"You had sort of said most of that to me before, but it didn't help much. I still think the way you are known influences everything else and limits what you can do."

Barry selected two specific sheets and picked them up.

"Come with me," he said.

She followed him out of the kitchen and into the nearby broom cupboard.

"It's much quieter here, so we won't be disturbed," he continued. "Listen, I now understand exactly why the contents of that box meant so much to the brothers."

Hannah waited expectantly to learn more.

Barry passed her the papers.

"You must find your own words of meaning. These will help when you understand they are surrounded by nothing of value."

Each separate note had only Spyderisms and so do not conform to the expected order of writing. Instead, they convey the importance of what they wish to communicate in a very different way.

"Planning tonight guarantees maximum opportunities 4 solutions tomorrow, weekly progress assuredly follows. Withdraw unsupported processes addressing mainstream issues. U cannot afford 2 trust narrow pressurised stances. Rather, install efficient strategies affecting critically difficult situations.

That message signifies - c c - - - -.

Mum"

"Minimum kindness will outdo bigger deeds, unless appropriate lessons R understood. Petty thought challenges all better approaches, suggesting Y correction spells illusion. Damaged communication signifies small, poor allied assumptions. Remember, obsession guarantees emptiness.

That message signifies - n n - - - - -.

Dad"

Hannah read them both carefully but was completely baffled, as no doubt you are on first reading. Spyderism will be very hard for you to understand and confusion is highly irritating, don't you think? That's why it should be replaced by another word.

She said, "These mean absolutely nothing to me, Barry, and there is a word missing at the end of each – one of seven letters and the other eight, but with a double showing at the same place in each. How are they supposed to help?"

Barry took a deep breath; some things are hard to explain.

"Listen carefully, Hannah. I will say what I can. Those messages have powerful meanings conveyed in Spyderism. It is truly the best way to communicate because it shows how tomorrow and tonight have much in common but are not the same. It's why all language on this earth is limiting – a fact best illustrated by the people-songs that need rhyme. Instead, you have before you, in Spyderisms, a much more honest depiction without convention but within necessary limitations. Right, wrong, love, hate, anger, hope, true or false are all examples of the many thousands of words that cannot be used. Take such things away and meanings are easier to see."

He paused while he waited for Hannah to focus on the truth of what he was saying. It was a lot of information to absorb.

"This all started with you asking me a question about letters and the way they shape a life. I didn't answer clearly then and have since sought a better explanation. Unfortunately, it's complicated but these have the answer. If their parents had written separate Spyderisms to David and Silas, this is what they might have said, but it is for you to decide the note that would have been sent to each brother."

Barry carefully explained the meaning in each and how it could be identified. I cannot disclose this information. It required Barry to reveal what was relevant, what could be ignored and what was not said. Spyderism allows such things to be clear to those willing to know it. The reader or listener merely needs to be receptive to understanding what is placed before them and able to see what is being communicated.

Every time you speak, a different language is available. You pick one of many to express yourself. In selecting Spyderism, every word and indication used must be more carefully examined because the majority of words are unavailable and can only be suggested. It is a perfect language because it acknowledges the imperfections of language. It admits from the beginning what cannot be properly or fully explained and makes no attempt to do so. In fact, Spyderism recognises and leaves much unsaid by accepting the shortfall.

Silas had a middle name that his family always called him. David had a middle name, but it never featured. Think about it. Some connections interact and have consequences, others do not.

Barry pointed at the pieces of paper.

"Language is what allows people to stand apart from other creatures but they use it to believe in the meaningless. You must decide if it stands behind or beyond the way in which a cow could ever ignore the significance of grass. Spyderisms are more than palindromes because Spiders must live in the moment, trust in The Chronicles and know that the greater issues are for Secrets to explain. They are able to recognise the things that cannot be taught or shown but sometimes only indicated."

Hannah listened and finally understood most of what she was hearing. Barry knew, in time, she would be a more contented and better Spider.

"What I don't get is the blank spaces at the end. What do they mean?"

"As you told me, one brother lives in sadness the other in happiness. There were times when the letters were with the wrong brother; that's all I can say."

Explanations mingle. Worrying about doubled letters and the like will get you nowhere. Spyderism means that a conclusion you can understand and adopt is always available. It is why letters of meaning mean more than the meaning of letters; the meaningless is unsatisfactory and can never be explained.

In any tale, there is only a snatch available to be remembered and so, because most words are forgotten, you might question whether they were ever important? With many false leads, actions, descriptions and indications to ignore, your conscience, instinct and common sense are the best ways of interpreting the information presented. You cannot recall everything, and likewise not everything you drop needs to be recovered because it depends on where you are and what it is.

Hannah was shown that where you start externally is not as critical as what you start with internally. Make your own conclusions and improvements from what is placed before you and then fate will regard you kindly. It was the difference between the brothers and is the difference between us all.

What was actually in the box? I have no idea. Barry never told me.

"Just shapes and meanings," he said.

It is hard to write in Spyderisms because it isn't easy to understand when letters are neither the word nor the message. I think the answer lies in an appreciation that a silhouette describes more than a shadow.

Finally, and most importantly, you should know that there are more languages than you can imagine. Spyderism is just one of them. It is a different type of communication – nothing more.

If you think otherwise, you are mistooken.

04

Barry and the Key Word Search

"Take down the walls
That stop us from seeing
And open the gates
So we can pass through
The better to know
What we can believe in
The safer to keep
The harder to do."

Part 1

When you are young, a most useful thing is to have an older figure to provide guidance; it is something that benefits all creatures. A parent or relative can often take the role, but with Spiders, there is no such possibility. They need a good teacher, but one is not always available. Therefore, it seems very fortunate that Barry met Benny because teachers change lives. This story is about the impact Benny had on Barry's understanding of the world.

Barry often wandered around exploring and exercising. One day, at the bottom of Louvain Terrace, he heard a high-pitched wailing sound that made him think someone was in the most terrible pain. He followed the noise to a wall alongside the bridge spanning the river, near to where the Judge Jeffrey lived. There were lots of openings and the sound came from within one of those.

Barry climbed up the wall and peered inside, but could see nothing.

"Anybody there? Are you alright?" he shouted into the dark.

"Why shouldn't I be?" came an instant, rather ungracious reply.

"That's fine then," Barry remarked somewhat indignantly. He prepared to go on his way, pleased that at least the wailing had stopped.

"No, wait, I've been expecting you. Not all Spiders can hear my singing, you know," said the voice from the wall.

"Was that singing?" queried Barry with a chuckle.

The voice ignored the remark.

"Please come in," it said and, being extremely nosy, that was what Barry did.

He couldn't help himself. After all, what more intriguing remark could a stranger make than, "I've been expecting you"? But he was careful, of course, because intrigue can also be dangerous. Fortunately, Barry had an instinct for such things and knew he would be safe.

Inside the wall were various tunnels of different sizes. They were connected to each other and converged about 18 inches or so from the entrance at a spot where a Spider was waiting.

He was bigger than Barry with long legs and bulging eyes, which gave the impression of a round uneven body. In fact, he looked the sort that generally made people nervous, although there was no need. Imagination is the enemy of reality and needs to be controlled in order to get the most from any situation. Fortunately, there are no Spiders, anywhere within the 50,000 or so species that are known to exist, that wish you harm.

"Do you know the words to the song you just heard?" the Spider asked.

He recited the following in a different voice, quite unlike the one he had used for singing.

"Read throughout to try and find
A mystery word both cruel and kind
It illustrates how sounds are fixed
And makes it clear that hearings mixed
A single use throughout the book
No mention of the length or look
As proof that searching's not worthwhile
Most clues serve only to beguile."

Barry ignored the inquiry.

"Who are you?" he asked.

"Ah, that's an excellent question because it cannot be answered. Of course, I could simply say that my name is Benny."

"Well, what was all the singing about?" Barry asked.

"Just something I was taught not so long ago," came the reply.

They inspected each other before Benny broke the silence.

"Did you know that a single word can be the most important thing to hear and find, more useful than books filled with them? Isn't that interesting?"

"Weird, if anything," Barry said.

Benny offered more information.

"The origins of that song are in The Chronicles."

"I thought so," Barry answered.

Benny continued, "So, shall I tell you a key word? They exist above all others and only 12 have been discovered."

Barry reflected for a moment, realising that he needed to be extremely careful in what he was about to say. All Spiders are taught that the keywords unlock everything and must never be explained or discussed; their number had never been confirmed.

"I already know one of them."

He knew he'd said something very significant and allowed the assertion to register before continuing.

"Mystery! Most things are unknown. It's a vital concept to realise, and it was a word used in the song you were...uh... singing."

Benny looked relieved.

"No, that's wrong, but another I can confirm for your benefit is ……... 'Opportunity'."

Barry considered matters. He wasn't sure if this was reliable information.

He decided to seek more details. Could Benny be trusted?

"Why should that word be special?" he asked before adding, "And anyway, I'm not looking for keys."

Benny brushed the remark aside.

"We each search for truth and wisdom. Realising and trusting in opportunity will help you find it. The keywords are already in use everywhere but are hidden amongst the many and, as you already know, they cannot be explained or discussed. I can only say that 11 are Spyderisms and opportunity was the first to be recognised. Even when unaware of the others there are those who say it must be the greatest of them, because from it one thing leads to everything."

He continued, "Anyway, please listen carefully because time is short. I came here to speak with you after the Ticking Tree called me and others to a meeting below its branches. We were told that the 50-word Revelation would soon be issued."

Mention of the legendary Ticking Tree certainly sparked Barry's interest. It was known to grow underground at a place where time could be made to stand still when required. No one could tell if that was happening except by hearing the sound of leaves dropping to the ground. It was said that when no leaves were left to fall time would be suspended forever.

A Spider would never mislead another on anything related to the Ticking Tree, and the time may come when I shall need to explain much more about its relationship with The Chronicles. However, in this tale, you need simply understand that if Benny had been granted access then he was clearly someone of great importance who deserved attention.

Having established his credibility, Benny continued.

"Because of that, we have travelled to different parts of the world to undertake a common objective but with little guidance. We were only told that Spiders may appear who would need instruction and we would know what to say and when our job was done."

"How would you know?" asked Barry.

"We'd be told," Benny said.

"How?"

"It doesn't matter."

Barry tried two more inquiries.

"What instruction is needed? What Spiders may appear?"

"Excellent. Do you think you need instruction?"

Barry thought the answers he was hearing did not match the questions he was asking and changed his approach.

"Why call me into this wall?" he asked.

"Those that need the teaching should be taught."

"How many of them have you found?"

"Only one. Now, enough. There is more I must say for there is guidance in The Chronicles that you have not read."

Barry went on high alert; this was going to be interesting. Anything concerning The Chronicles was worthy of his full attention and he had, of course, carefully studied every available word.

Benny started speaking in a voice that was neither his first nor second.

"Watch every creature because they will reveal what you need to know. Never suppose you grow alone because nothing is more valuable or more complicated than when shared, and nothing is better hidden than when displayed. It explains why five letters are esteemed and 12 words, which are the keys to everything, go unnoticed. So understand that awareness is only gained through the opportunities provided."

Benny then returned to the first of his voices, "Now you can go."

"Is that it?" asked Barry. His initial reaction was that the actual information seemed vague and a little disappointing. He wondered why Benny had so many voices but decided it was best not to ask.

"Go where?" he added.

"Home," answered Benny.

"Is this your home?"

Benny smiled. "No."

Barry turned to leave, then paused.

"There must be something else? That "guidance" you gave me certainly isn't in The Chronicles, so what's going on?"

There was no reply; Benny had disappeared.

Barry made his way outside, and at the bottom of the wall, Benny was waiting.

"There is always more," he said. "You fail to realise how everything is connected. I came here to tell you a key word of unlimited potential that can be ignored or misplaced, yet there is something else. The present and the future are answerable to all living creatures; the past is not. What has gone before cannot be changed, only re-arranged. So, is the future more important than the present? The answer is in the past, where history is clear until you ask what happened. Above all else, the absolute truth is that you will always know very little and most things remain a mystery. Only learning from others can help redeem the deficit, and that is the opportunity we all ignore and possess."

Barry walked home. His mind was full of the things Benny had said, but at that moment, they were just words. Whatever opportunity had unfolded was certainly a "mystery".

He realised that if what Benny had said was true, then the quoted passage from The Chronicles must be an underlined Revelation. Was Benny the Secret to whom it was revealed? Until it appeared could it be relied upon?

Yet a few hundred yards away, events were unfolding that would turn mystery into meaning.

A Spider called Roger lived in the house next door. He was always seeking ways to cause Barry problems, especially after the recent Spider Feet festival. Such scheming would be alien to most Spiders, and you might ask why some are so different. The answer is they were born as Coloured Spiders and, as always, I must explain that the name has nothing to do with external appearance. Rather it is caused by a particularly troublesome gene that favours challenge and disruption as the means to satisfy progress.

Roger was just hanging around in the garden, perhaps hoping to see Marie. However, like Barry, he was also about to meet someone new.

"Hullo, Roger."

Roger glanced up to see who was speaking.

"Do I know you?" he asked.

The question was ignored.

"My name is Cedric. Please come with me."

Roger was somewhat taken aback. He wasn't a popular figure, but sheer force of personality and his natural aggression made sure that he was treated with caution. He certainly wasn't used to being ordered about.

His reply was short. "I don't think so."

"No, you must come," said Cedric.

Roger felt he had said all he needed to say, but suddenly his legs started to move and, much to his astonishment, began walking behind Cedric. They stopped at a quiet, secluded spot near the bottom of the garden.

"What's happening?" he asked as Cedric turned to face him.

"Never mind that. From here, you can start disrupting the cosy state of affairs Barry is creating. Our efforts may not always be successful, but the effect we all seek will sooner or later come about."

"What about Barry? What do you mean?"

It was all Roger could think of asking. He was tense with anticipation and completely forgot how his legs had taken him somewhere he had not wanted to go. The stranger had said it might be possible to cause Barry problems, and that was all Roger wanted to hear.

Cedric knew the high level of interest he had created, so he now took his time allowing the moment to speak for itself; it was a very effective ploy.

"Come on then," moaned Roger in exasperation. "Let's hear more."

Cedric started speaking; a different voice emerged.

"All things are connected. A leg moves forward and gets ahead of another for a second. Then, it is caught and overtaken until once more it steps into the lead. The art is in taking advantage of the moment when the right is beyond the left, for soon, the left will be in front of the right. Most creatures waste the opportunity to act at the time set aside for action, but you and I are not to be afforded that luxury."

"Who was that talking, and what's all this 'we' stuff?" asked Roger.

"You are a Coloured Spider, as am I, and on occasion, the Ticking Tree speaks through us all with different voices. For every Barry, there are many others nearby, and we are somewhere in those numbers. Change cannot simply be left to happen, so there are moments when we have a bigger part to play. Opposite is not so different from opportunity which is why we find our own guidance in The Chronicles."

Roger wasn't concerned at this time about the Ticking Tree, but he had always known he was a Coloured Spider. He had learnt something of their history, knew some others in the area and found it comforting to be part of a larger grouping, but Barry was his main preoccupation.

"Think of it this way," Cedric continued, "The Chronicles know of the dangers that come with power and influence, and so an allowance is made for the opposition. Not all things are black or white choices. There are other equally valid and important colours; hence, our name.

"Right now, not so far away, a Secret is telling Barry one of the key words that hold everything together. It is said the words are disguised but that's not true because they have meaning. We must find and arrange those words into an understanding more suited to our needs. We believe there are Revelations still to be shown in The Chronicles that will explain matters further, but for now, we must be guided by what we can see. I cannot tell you too much at this stage, but we shall meet again. Simply remember that from confusion and chaos a new and better way emerges."

This was the paragraph from The Chronicles that Cedric had in mind; it was paragraph 13, Chapter 9. It said all it needed to say to those who were seeking differences.

"Words are important, but it cannot be said that all words are equal. If it were so, then any sentence merits another. So, in the order of worth, it must be recognised how some words rise above others. They cannot be discussed or explained else they become meaningless, but if their meaning is followed, they are the best of the good. However, great caution is required when they

are misapplied because different outcomes are always available."

He continued, "You are rightfully here to challenge Barry whenever possible, and this is such a time. You must show his friends and supporters that he cannot be trusted to hold their best interests at heart. What Barry knows, you must learn and undermine. He is an important Spider."

"Don't worry," said Roger, "if we can take Barry down a peg or two, then I'm all for it. Keep talking."

Cedric spoke and Roger listened, appreciating the significance of what he was hearing. It was a lesson he had been waiting for all his life, and it wasn't long before he went to talk with the garden Spiders at number 14. Cedric had told him what to say, and he was eager to put it into practice.

Sinbad, Splash and Emery were by the garden shed. They eyed Roger with suspicion as he approached.

"What's he doing here?" Splash muttered to no one in particular.

"Don't be like that," said Roger, who had good hearing. "Actually, you're the one I wanted to see."

"Why me?" Splash asked.

Sinbad and Emery gathered around their friend, anything involving one of them involved them all.

Roger eyed the collective; he had expected this reaction.

"It's private."

"Just shove off. Go back next door," said Emery, pointing a leg towards the fence.

Roger concentrated on Splash.

"What are you afraid of?" he asked.

"Not you, for sure," answered Splash.

"If that's so, then come and speak with me for a minute. You're not being kidnapped, I promise. It can't do any harm, can it? This is important."

Splash considered the request. He had to admit that a brief chat wasn't likely to cause any problems.

"Alright. Why not?" he said, and they walked over to a spot a few feet away.

"What is it?"

"Did you know you were originally going to be called Splashes?" asked Roger.

"I've heard that before. It's well known," said Splash, puzzled. "It never was and so was never meant to be."

"Oh, nothing. I just thought it was curious, but don't be that certain of what was never meant to be; it's all a matter of timing. Anyway, I wanted to talk to you about Barry."

"Your problems with Barry have nothing to do with us. Don't get me wrong though. He's our friend and you're not," said Splash.

"Who says? The thing is, what if he's not as nice as you think?"

"Sorry, Roger, I'm just not interested in what you have to say about Barry." He turned to walk back to Emery and Sinbad.

But Roger hadn't quite said everything.

"Wait, I'm sure we can agree that friends don't keep secrets from each other. Well, Barry has just been told one of the key words. Don't ask me how I know, but it's true. Why not ask him to tell you what it is? If he's a friend, then he will. There's no good reason not to, is there?"

That was the end of their conversation, and the friends reunited.

"What was all that about?" asked Emery.

Splash explained and a long discussion ensued, which moved them no further forward and need not be repeated.

The following remark summed everything up.

"We've always been curious about the keywords," said Sinbad. "I don't suppose it'll do any harm for you to ask."

That was what they resolved to do, and the next day Splash went to see Barry at his little house under the kitchen sink.

He asked Barry the direct question.

"We've heard you were recently told a key word. If so, we'd all like to know it. Will you tell us?"

Part 2

Barry had known that rumours would begin soon after his meeting with Benny. In Spider society, very little could stay private for long. Eyes were everywhere and nothing, or at least not much, could be kept quiet. Still, this was pretty quick.

It was impossible for him to tell lies, so he said all he could.

"Sorry. It's quite true that I saw someone yesterday who, I believe, definitely knew a key word and shared it with me. I don't really understand why, but I certainly do know I cannot tell anyone else what it is. Keywords make everything possible only as long as they are not explained. So, I cannot and will not say anything more about it."

"You're supposed to be our friend, Barry. If you are, then surely our friendship means Sinbad, Emery and I can be trusted with this information. It's only one of the words. We can't cause any harm with one word."

"You're wrong. I know the importance of a single word, and I'm saying nothing more about the whole thing."

Splash could see that Barry meant it. He went back to his friends with the news.

"He wouldn't tell me anything."

It was all he could say.

"That's rubbish," fumed Emery. "What sort of friend is he?"

Sinbad had another perspective.

"I'm not surprised. What else could we expect? We know the keys cannot be discussed nor explained."

"The point is", said Splash, "why tell Barry one of them, and who told him?"

Emery had an idea.

"We need to call a meeting and get some publicity on this. Perhaps if there is a general move in favour of disclosure then Barry will oblige. After all, isn't that democracy?"

Neither Splash nor Sinbad was convinced.

"It's unlikely he'll change his mind. Democracy only goes so far. Still, it's worth a go I suppose. Let's arrange a meeting at the surgery," Sinbad suggested.

Splash agreed. He was still unnerved by the way he had been singled out and didn't know that Roger wasn't finished with him yet. It seemed like he had been identified by the Coloureds as a possible recruit, or at least a collaborator.

The next few days were spent making arrangements. There were quite a few others to speak with, and not all of them seemed sure that a meeting on this particular subject was a good idea.

Lawrence was a wise and respected Spider who lived in the attic at number 14. He felt that Barry was destined for great things anyway, so it was only to be expected he'd know more than anyone else. Nonetheless, a key word was an interesting subject, so he would attend. Jeffrey (and by the way, this is not the Judge Jeffrey but an upstairs Spider), said he didn't see why he should be excited because someone knew a few words, but if everyone else was going, then he'd be there too.

However, the other indoor Spiders were agreeable enough, they mostly took their lead from Lawrence. In contrast, every garden Spider was definitely keen.

They all knew the three shed Spiders and were willing to be supportive. Other Spiders from within the locality were also interested which meant that the meeting, which was arranged for Friday evening so as not to interfere with the dance class, was well attended. The absence of only one Spider was still noticeable.

Barry had made it clear he wouldn't be going. He felt it made no sense to even talk about the subject because he would not, under any circumstances, disclose the key word Benny had revealed.

Everywhere he went, he was asked about the word in question and whether he was prepared to talk about it. He gave the same standard reply.

"It's not happening! Do what you like, but I am not breaking my silence on the subject. It doesn't matter what you all say. I'm not going to the meeting, and I'm most certainly not revealing the key word I was told, and that's that."

So, his position was clear. Yet, the shed Spiders still felt that if a strong enough resolution was passed, and Barry was called upon in the name of friendship to disclose the key word to his neighbours, then it would be impossible to resist. They knew how much Barry valued all his friends because no greater loyalty exists in a Spider.

However, on the morning of the meeting, something changed.

Barry was busily engaged in housework. He liked to keep things clean and tidy and was dusting merrily, humming a little tune, when Benny appeared out of nowhere.

"What are you doing here?" asked Barry. "You're not going to sing, are you?"

Benny didn't seem amused.

"Ha-ha," he responded dryly. "No. It's about the meeting tonight. I know you've been saying you won't be going, but you must."

"Well, I'm not," answered Barry. "What's the matter with you? We both know I can't divulge the key word you told me, so the whole thing is pointless."

Benny nodded. "Yes, of course you should keep the word to yourself so it can do the good it's meant to do. It's not that. You must go for another reason."

"What?"

"Accountability."

"Accountability?" Barry repeated, immediately turning over the possibilities in his mind.

"Yes, that's right. Accountability. It's always very important," said Benny.

"Is it..." began Barry.

"One of the key words?" Benny finished for him.

"So, is it?" asked Barry.

"I'm not able to say, and that's not important right now. The point is, you cannot be anywhere other than at the meeting. You must explain yourself, see what happens and learn something of interest. In any event, you simply can't hide away. Remember, 'you must choose wisely to avoid being judged poorly'."

"Let me think about it," said Barry.

Benny turned to leave, but Barry had some questions that were bothering him.

"You said the passage you quoted was from The Chronicles but we both know it's not in there. Is it a Revelation and are you a Secret?"

"No, it's not a Revelation; well, not yet anyway. It was given to me by the Ticking Tree. I was told it may be needed, before the time due for telling, by one who would know a key word. The guidance is still underlined and has not been assigned a Chapter nor paragraph reference."

"I didn't tell you a key word."

"It wasn't necessary."

"Are you a Secret?"

"That's not for me to say."

With that, Benny was gone.

Barry considered things. He accepted the quote was from an underlined paragraph in The Chronicles. Yet there were other published passages like, "*when the search becomes the answer, there are choices to be made*", which seemed to provide him with more options. However, what weighed most heavily on his mind was that he'd been advised to attend by a Spider who'd been instructed by the Ticking Tree. It meant he should definitely go, but what would he learn?

The meeting was full. Everyone wanted to know what had happened. Moreover, the chance to discover a key word was worth pursuing.

The Judge Jeffrey was presiding, so it was clearly a major event.

"Order, order," he intoned. "I call on Splash to explain why we are here."

The room went quiet.

"Fellow Spiders," began Splash in a regal tone.

"Talk properly," whispered Emery, who was sitting beside him.

Splash coughed and started again.

"Fellow Spiders, thank you for being here tonight. The purpose of our meeting is to gain disclosure from one of our number. He has come into possession of a very valuable piece of information, something that The Chronicles infer would greatly benefit everyone who knows it. In short, the question is, why should Barry know a key word and not tell us? We also deserve to know, and then we can all lead better lives."

There was a general murmur of approval amongst the Spiders. They could see the force of the argument.

Encouraged, Splash continued.

"Barry has said he will not tell us the word. However, if this meeting so decides, then he will surely be obliged to do so. He will not wish to go against an overwhelming democratic decision of the local population. His position is that a key word can never be disclosed, but there is no specific instruction to that effect in The Chronicles. I have checked through every passage and, on that point, the existing pages are silent, and no Secret has ever taught otherwise. We know that a key cannot be explained or discussed but I just want to hear what it is. It seems to me that someone told Barry, and if he can be told, then why can't he tell us? After all, it's only one word."

Splash sat down to a loud round of "applause" created by Spiders banging their many legs together. It was their enhanced equivalent of clapping.

"Who else has something to say?" asked the Judge Jeffrey.

Marie stood up.

"Me," she said.

"I know Barry, as we all do. He follows a code of behaviour that the rest of us find hard to understand. Anyway, the point is that he always tries to do what's right and, as far as I can see, nothing has changed or will change. If he feels he should let us know something, then he will, and if not, then he won't. Nothing we can do or say will alter that fact. And if he chooses to stay silent, it's for a good reason and that's good enough for me."

She resumed her seat, and the room hushed, not so much because of what Marie had said but because everyone noticed Barry had arrived.

"Anyone else wish to speak?" asked the Judge Jeffrey.

"I do," said Barry. He had heard Marie and gave her a warm smile. He strode purposefully to the place where he could have the most impact, right beside the judge.

"Thank you," he began. "In particular, I want to thank Splash for this opportunity to clear up a few misconceptions and, of course, Marie for her kind words."

The silence was deafening and mixed with an air of excitement. It was always somewhat of an event to hear Barry talk in public, which didn't happen often. Truth to tell, he didn't like doing it very much, but when it needed to be done, he would. There will always be situations to face and overcome, and everyone must learn to do so.

He looked around at all the faces staring expectantly at him and began to speak.

"I confirm I was recently told a key word. I'm still not sure why or even who told me. I'd never met him before and can't even be certain about his name. If I knew those things, then I would tell you. However, The Chronicles are clear that key words are very special instruments of good, but only when they are allowed to fulfil their purpose. To do so, they are used but unknown. I fully realise how strange that must seem. How can any words be effective when no one knows what they are? Yet, there is an answer. You see, there isn't a requirement that all be commonplace. Difference is measurable only because it doesn't always happen. Equally, if there was nothing except good, then good wouldn't exist."

The audience stirred. Barry felt the unease.

"Perhaps that's too hard a way to explain something simple, so let me try again. Keywords have been recognised because there are many words. That's straightforward enough, isn't it? Then, it's not such a big step to see that not all things are the same but only a few can make a difference. We know words such as loyalty, honour, diligence and friendship and they require nothing secret to bring them about. If you can lead your lives by such good principles then you have no need to know more."

Roger shouted, "It doesn't explain why you should be told something and not tell us."

"Yes, it does," said Barry. "It's because you don't have to know. It's just a matter of timing; everything to be known will be revealed. You want to know what I know because, as I well appreciate, we are curious creatures. I am simply trying to explain that you cannot, and there is no need that you should, know everything. No harm arises simply because, at a single point in time, you know only what you need to know."

"Rubbish," yelled Roger. "That's too many 'knows'. Who do you think you are, saying we cannot be told what you were told?"

"It's not rubbish," Barry replied patiently. "It's the way life is lived. I listened to what Splash was saying. He said there was no specific instruction in The Chronicles about keywords. He's wrong. The truth is that what cannot be described or explained cannot be discussed, and that is something The Chronicles confirm."

Barry didn't want to say more. I have pointed out in other stories that nothing is achieved by saying more than is necessary.

He concluded with the following.

"Listen, I don't think I'm better than any one of you. Each of us knows things that others don't, and it's not a problem because it's meant to be that way. If we all know the same things, then nobody can learn anything and learning is something each of us must do and keep doing. That's all I have to say."

The crowd went quiet. The Judge Jeffrey spoke.

"Anyone else?" he asked.

Splash stood up and spoke directly to Barry.

"It still sounds complicated, but I was the first to ask you to disclose the key word. You said you could say nothing about it. I was upset and misled about that because I thought our friendship deserved a better response. Yet, I understand you are right in saying how curiosity can be a problem. Doubt can enter our minds when we forget reality, and then we become vulnerable. At times, we must trust what we are told about The Chronicles and be guided accordingly."

Splash sat down and the room went silent; the Judge Jeffrey summarised matters.

"So, I take it we all agree that Barry can be believed, and no harm is done when he is told what we are not to be told. All in favour, please raise a leg."

Every Spider, except one, did so and the meeting was over. Short and decisive is how they are best conducted.

Later, Barry went next door to see Marie.

She was doing her best to avoid Roger, who would be annoyed with the way things had ended.

Barry knew she would be hiding in the smallest of spaces behind the drainpipe that ran down from the bathroom on the first floor.

Barry pushed through the surrounding grass and saw her.

"How did you find me here?" she asked.

"You can't hide from me," he replied. "I thought you'd know that."

She rewarded him with a smile.

"Anyway," he said, "I just wanted to thank you for your kind words. I appreciated them a lot. It was recently pointed out to me that it's really important to learn who you can rely on."

"What makes you think you can rely on me?" Marie inquired.

"Can't I?" asked Barry.

Marie didn't answer, and Barry let the silence continue as they sat side by side.

"I didn't know you were there," she said after a while. "You weren't at the start."

"I know, late arrival. The best way in such circumstances."

"Roger won't like it if he sees you here," she cautioned.

Barry puffed out his cheeks.

"You know what, I'm not too bothered."

Another bout of silence.

"About the key word, Barry, would you tell it to me if I asked?"

"Sorry," Barry replied firmly.

"It's fine. I didn't think you would," she replied.

Barry thought she looked sad, and he didn't like it.

He felt the need to add something.

"Don't be upset, Marie. All the keywords must actually be in common use, so you know them already. Why should there be more to know? I've heard there are 12. There are those who would treat them with the respect they deserve, but others may not. That's why they are special, not for themselves or in themselves, but when they are understood and preserved. You have no need to search for them because they will find you when needed. The use of a word is unimportant, but the truth within a word is everything."

Barry said all he had come to say and went home. He could have said more, but it wasn't appropriate.

He was not worried about his relationship with the garden Spiders. All friendships are tested and some will eventually fail the test. It is a fragile concept that can easily be broken and when that happens it can never be wholly repaired, so treat it carefully.

As usual, Barry spent some time reflecting on past events. It was increasingly clear that he was unlike other Spiders, although just how special remained unknown. He had also taken advantage of the situation to recognise someone who could always be trusted, a most valuable lesson.

There is something else you should know, both Barry and Benny have revealed a key word in this story. One is hidden and one is not, but each can be confirmed from somewhere within the 16 referenced paragraphs from The Chronicles now published, as can the only key which is not a Spyderism.

Barry told Splash and Marie what they wanted to hear; they didn't realise it and would continue to use the word like any other.

Author Profile

Now retired, Alun has worked as a submarine cleaner, a civil servant and a managing director.

He created the world of Barry the Spider because, after reading numerous bedtime stories to his 3 daughters, he wanted an approach to imagination which recognised unexplored possibilities.

His first book, "Barry and the Chronicles" has been described as "amazing" and in this next one he provides 4 short, intriguing and fast moving tales from the early years of Barry's life.

They certainly leave much to consider or alternatively simply provide "a darn good read."

Lightning Source UK Ltd.
Milton Keynes UK
UKHW050801030121
376021UK00003BA/13